MA[illegible]

T[illegible]IG

MOUNTAIN

MAN

IRIS WEST

CHAPTER ONE

Keisha

AS THE MOUNTAINS of Blossom Ford, Arizona, come into view, my heart settles down a little. They look as breathtaking as they did in the photos Barret sent. I might be taking the greatest risk of my life, but at least I'll be doing it in a place that sings to my soul.

I signed up to Blossom Ford Matchmaking Agency's Mail-Order bride program on a whim, still, deciding to marry Barrett came from a place inside that connected with the type of person he is. My lips tilt up as I remember the words he used to introduce himself:

"I'm a big, callous ridden, rough around the edges man. Your life will be hard, but you'll have the satisfaction of knowing you've worked hard for your keep and the solace of being among nature's beauty. I can't give you sweet words, however you can expect a committed and hard-working man who'll provide for our family."

The words and their tone told me so much about my prospective husband.

He's offering what I'm searching for. A lasting marriage based on mutual trust, understanding and a will to make it work.

I've experienced first-hand the hurt and betrayal a passionate relationship brings and have decided to have nothing to do with it.

Mom and Dad were so happy in the early years of my life, I thought I was the luckiest girl alive. By the time I got to middle school, I stayed out as much as possible to avoid the arguing. They are the best of friends now, but before they divorced, my lovely parents had turned into two warring enemies.

Despite being jaded, I tried dating. I figured what I'd learned from seeing my parents fight and my desire and determination to have a healthy relationship gave me an advantage. It took forever to find a boyfriend. It turns out not many guys want to date a girl who's taller and bigger than them.

Eventually, I found someone who I thought might be the man of my dreams. It didn't last long.

"Baby, expecting me to sleep only with you is unreasonable. I thought you understood I'm a free guy. And I like variety," he'd said when I caught him cheating with a girl at least three times skinnier than me.

I hadn't understood. After that, I just couldn't bring myself to believe in passionate love. The pain of being in love didn't seem worth it to me.

Someone at work mentioned modern mail-order brides, horrified at the idea of a loveless marriage. The more I thought about it, the more sense it made sense. After I turned twenty-five and was made redundant for the second time in my life, I looked into it and came across Barrett's profile.

The train slows as it eases into Blossom Ford. I get up and gather my rucksack and suitcase. I'm about to open the door when it's wrenched back. A word of thanks is on the tip of my tongue when a huge hand reaches out and effortlessly lifts my suitcase down before I can reach it.

"Thank you," I say after I exit the train. I gaze up and up. It's an unusual thing for me. Being nearly six feet, I'm the person who usually looks down. He must be at least six feet four. A thrill runs through me. I'm such a sucker for tall men.

"Hi Keisha. I'm Barret."

His profile picture doesn't do him justice.

He's not a pretty man, yet I've met no one hotter. Thick, arched eyebrows frame his hazel eyes. A brown beard flanks lips meant to bring pleasure to a woman. Shoulder-length chestnut hair with blonde highlights reaches the top of his shoulders.

Heat flushes my cheeks. I realize I've ignored his outstretched hand while ogling him and flush again.

I've always thought of my hands as huge, but my hand feels tiny in his much larger one.

All the chit chat I prepared vanishes from my mind, butterflies fill my tummy.

"It's nice to meet you," my voice is annoyingly croaky.

"You too. Let me take your rucksack."

"It's alright, I can carry it."

"You look like you can, but you've been traveling for hours. It's no trouble to me." He stretches his hand out like he won't accept no for an answer.

I'm so used to taking care of my own things, I'm ruffled for a moment. But then I remind myself I decided to embrace this new life.

I pass him the heavy bag and watch as he lugs it onto his back like it weighs nothing.

A whistle rings.

"Come on, the train is about to depart."

I follow Barrett down the platform, startled to notice I am the only person to get off the train.

There's a small parking lot outside with two trucks. Barrett leads me to the oldest one and as he stows my luggage in the trunk, I glance toward the sprawling town. Just breathing the air makes me feel good. I close my eyes and look up at the sky, luxuriating in the hot rays of the sun.

"Great, isn't it?"

My eyes fly open. Barrett is facing the mountains, admiration and pride emanating from his easy stance.

"I can feel the difference in air quality between here and Garnet City."

He goes to the passenger side and opens the door.

Something warm moves in my chest.

It's not just because I can't remember if any man has ever done that for me, it's the casual way he opens the door, like that's how he was brought up. It's so unlike his description of himself.

I get in the truck and watch as Barret closes the door and stalks around to the driver's seat. His height, burly chest and long legs as thick as tree trunks don't stop him from moving gracefully.

"Do you want to grab a quick bite before we head to the registry office?"

"I had a snack on the train."

I washed my face and freshened my makeup, too. Even though I am a cleanser and cream only girl, I plan on getting married only once; I want to look my best.

My ivory dress reaches just above my knees and shows my curves to what I hope is perfection. I had my hair pressed at the hairdressers yesterday and took great care to make sure it doesn't frizz. I swapped my heels for sneakers during my journey, but changed again when I freshened up.

"I was expecting more luggage," Barrett says as he heads away from the train station.

"Disappointed?"

"Hell no! If anything, I'm in awe."

"Clothes shopping is not a favorite. I keep a couple

of nice dresses, but the rest of my clothes are jeans."

"I'm the same, so I'm glad to hear that."

"You have a couple of dresses too?"

Barrett chuckles. The sound is big and booming like him.

My heart skips a beat at the way his face transforms. He looks younger, more approachable.

As we drive through town, Barret points out places I might need to visit. He stops the truck after only a ten-minute ride outside an imposing building.

"We're here." He switches off the engine of the powerful car and faces me. "It's not too late to change your mind."

There's a steadiness in his voice that calms me. I'm surer now than when I left the city I grew up in.

"I'm sure."

I return his gaze, wanting him to see how determined I am.

When I responded to his request, he'd written back, saying I was too young to settle into the hard life of the mountain and he was too old for me. It took a lot to convince him my twenty-five years of age didn't diminish my desire for the type of life he was offering and that his age was a plus for me. I enjoyed living in the city, but I wouldn't miss it. I wanted a mature man who was ready to settle down, not a younger man not ready to be exclusive.

He nods and I sigh.

After he climbs out of the truck, I check my makeup one more time, reminding myself Barrett Montgomery is the man I decided to marry with a contract in order to build a strong marriage and a family. Passion doesn't come into it. Attraction is fine, it'll help things in the bedroom. However, falling in love is forbidden.

The success of this marriage is important to me. If I'm the only one who falls in love and Barret finds out, it might invalidate our contract. And that's something I don't want. So I tell my heart to stop being moved by his gentlemanly behavior and kindness.

CHAPTER TWO

Barrett

I'M DOING THE right thing, I tell myself as I stand beside Keisha in one of the registry office rooms, waiting for the officiant to start the wedding ceremony. This is the best way to ensure what happened to Dad doesn't happen to me.

I thought I was over my childish desire for a large family of my own, however the last few years I've longed for companionship, someone to share my evenings with. I resisted the urge for so long, but I guess what my grandaddy and the townsfolk used to say about Montgomery men not being able to live on their own is true after all.

Grandaddy also used to say Montgomery men fall head over heels with one woman only and love her despite how cruel she might be. Dad loved Mom until his last day, even though she abandoned him a year after their marriage, when I was only three months old.

I'm making sure I don't lose my head over some woman who isn't suited for mountain living. I'm getting hitched on my own terms. With a partner who has the same values as I do and wants a lasting, solid marriage based on family.

It's just I didn't expect to be nervous. Maybe everyone gets nervous on their wedding day, whether or not they are in love.

Keisha certainly does. She's clasping the small bouquet in her hands as if it can hold her up. Yet she's standing straight, the determined look in her chocolate brown eyes and the tilt of her firm chin making me feel easier.

She's the most beautiful woman I've ever seen. I wasn't expecting a wedding gown. She's stunning in a simple ivory dress that reaches her elbows and knees. I'm used to towering over women, but the top of her silky head reaches my shoulders. It's the perfect height to pull her in close, kiss her bow shaped bottom lip and caress her delectable curves.

I'm grateful when Mr. Rose, the officiant, starts the ceremony and pulls my mind from the direction it's taking. I focus on the words he's saying. I'm only marrying once, and I intend to follow my vows.

"Barrett, do you take this woman to be your wife, to live together in matrimony, to love, honor and comfort her, in sickness and in health, forsaking all others, for as long as you both shall live?"

"Yes," I answer, my eyes on Keisha. The possessive tone of my voice surprises me, but I don't hide it. It's best she sees me for who I am.

Her gaze is steady on me as she accepts to take me as her husband.

She's mine the moment she says yes.

We exchange the gold rings I bought and the simple ceremony we both chose is over.

"You may kiss the bride."

I take Keisha's hands in mine, holding the flowers with her. The band on her ring finger glides against my rough palm. Her eyes widen.

I lean in, looking at her, and stop a breath from her mouth. She closes the distance between us.

Satisfaction and something else rise in me and I want to growl. The desire to taste her is so strong, I have to hold myself back, lest I scare her away.

I press my lips against hers. Softness and sweetness push back. It's the most innocent of touches yet, when I reluctantly pull back, it leaves me wanting more.

Mr. Rose insists on taking a couple of pictures in the sunny garden outside. He's not satisfied until Keisha and I have our arms around each other and are smiling at the camera.

"It was kind of the officiant to take a photo of us," Keisha says as we enter the car.

My lips tug up. "You mean interfering, right?"

"He was pushy, like a grandfather or an uncle. Is he

a family member?"

"He and Dad were school friends. Now Dad is not around anymore. Now and then, he feels like it's his place to make sure I'm doing the right thing."

Mr. Rose had always been like that, especially during the time I was younger.

"That's nice."

Is that longing in Keisha's voice?

"You might not think that when you can't go more than a few yards without someone asking how you are doing because they haven't seen you for a while. Most of the time, it's nosiness."

"I still think I'd prefer that to people not noticing my absence."

"Let's see how you feel in ten, twenty years."

Keisha looks at the bouquet in her hands. Her hair hides her face.

I fight the desire to pull that curtain of silk behind her ear and turn her toward me.

When she finally gazes at me, there's a smile around her lips and eyes.

"Let's."

"Do you want to go to a restaurant?"

Keisha bites her lip. "I can last a couple of hours if that's what you'd like to do, but I'd prefer to shower and wear something comfortable. These shoes are killing me."

I'm smiling from ear to ear. It was definitely the right decision to pick my life partner based on compatibility.

"Take them off."

Keisha bites her bottom lip again, two white teeth worrying the nude, perfect bow.

A bolt of desire shoots straight for my cock.

About to strip my suit jacket and tie, I change my mind and remove only the tie. I toss it to the back of the truck and leave my suit jacket to serve as cover for my groin.

Keisha slips her feet out of her ivory shoes and sighs.

"That bad?"

"It's hard to find shoes that fit. Even if they're the right size, they're uncomfortable soon after wearing them. I suppose trainers are okay for you. Do you have trouble getting formal shoes?"

"I only have a couple of pairs. I had them specially made."

Even sneakers were hard to find in my size. It used to bother me when I was in middle and high school. Not anymore. A few pairs of boots are all I need, anyway.

As I drive off toward the mountain, with Keisha sitting beside me, a feeling I can't place settles within me. I put it down to a sense of belonging with another person. I came down the mountain single. Now, I have a family, someone I'm responsible for.

I'm sure that's also what's got me wanting to whistle and is making the greenery on the mountain especially beautiful today.

"How long does it take to get to the top of the mountains? Have you tried it?"

"It depends on whether you go up the beaten track or take the routes only locals know. It can take the best part of a day or a few hours."

When I was younger, I used to go every time I fought with Dad.

"What happens if you're halfway up and it's nighttime? I'd be terrified in the woods at night."

"These woods are safer than many places. Most people go up on organized tours."

Keisha's gaze wanders, taking in everything around her.

My wife.

She wants the same things I do. Which is how I want it always to be. That's why that unfamiliar feeling in my chest can only be a sense of responsibility, belonging, and possession.

Whenever Dad got drunk, he'd talk about Mom. Reminisce over the early days of their marriage when Mom was still infatuated with the mountain. It was painful to watch. Mom's name was the last thing he said before he passed.

He never got over her. As a kid, I blamed him for not leaving with Mom. Now, I understand why he couldn't. These woods are part of me.

I'm already in lust with Keisha. Her intoxicating scent of mint, the warm tone of her mocha skin that seems to invite my touch, and her curvaceous body is playing havoc with my self-control.

I want my wife. There's nothing wrong with that.

I already like her inquisitive nature and respect her determination to make this marriage work, just like me, and that's fine, too. The only thing that would be wrong is falling head over heels for her. However, that will not happen, because my whole being knows better than to allow myself to go through what Dad did.

CHAPTER THREE

Keisha

WE PULL THROUGH a gate with the sign Montgomery Chicken Farm into a large yard. Barrett stops in front of a large wooden cabin. I recognize it from the photos he sent.

I unbuckle my seat belt and slip my shoes back on. Barrett swings my door open and I step down from the truck, bag on my shoulder.

"This is our home," he sounds gruff, yet I hear pride in his booming voice. Warmth spreads through me when I process the word our.

Without a warning, he picks me up. One moment I'm standing awkwardly in front of him and the next I'm being swept up into his arms, like a dainty damsel in distress.

Surprise has my arms locking around his neck. A

laugh escapes me.

Barret stalks toward the front door. Before I can fumble to open it, he shoves the door back with one foot.

"Welcome home, Mrs. Montgomery!"

I can't look away from him. I'm held in his hazel eyes, trapped by the promise of heat I see there. My heart beats faster. A bleat breaks the near silence in the yard.

"That's Angelina, the kindest of our goats. I guess she's welcoming you."

The spell is broken. Barrett puts me down.

As soon as his hands fall off my waist, I'm wanting them back there. Feeling hot and a little dazed, I wander around the living room of the wooden cabin. I need space away from Barrett.

There's a comfortable old sofa along one wall and an imposing, antique chest opposite it. A picture of a young-looking Barrett and a man sits proudly on it. There's another picture, but this was clearly taken at a family photo studio.

"Is this you?" I point to the baby in the studio photo.

He nods. "That's Dad and my mother."

"You were cute."

Barrett raises a bushy eyebrow. "That's past tense. Am I no longer cute?"

Is he kidding me? He's so cute right now, with his hands tucked into his trouser pockets and the ghost of a smile playing around his lips. I want to sidle up to him and kiss that raised eyebrow. Instead, I shrug.

"Your Mom is pretty. Do your parents live nearby?"

He removes his hands from his pant pockets.

"Dad passed a few years ago. Mom doesn't live around here." He walks toward the front door. "I'll grab your stuff."

I stare at his back as he marches outside.

***

AS I FINISH dressing, the sun is setting. I listen out for Barret, wondering if he is back from checking on the animals. One more glance in the mirror convinces me I've done everything possible to look good in a pair of my most comfortable yet sexy jeans and a V-neck top that shows my cleavage to its best.

I glance at the massive bed, my side of the closet, and my toiletries on the dresser. He must have more stuff than me, even so Barret left more than half of the space everywhere for me. I wanted a new start, so only brought what I thought would be useful here and sold the rest. My paltry belongings hardly cover the space he created for me.

The sheets on the bed and the curtains are old, but they are clean and pretty. It's comforting, knowing the furnishings in the cabin have been used by Barrett's ancestors, who are now my family.

The thought of sleeping with Barrett has me glancing at the bed again. Heat creeps up my cheeks when my core clenches. Alarmed, I accidentally slam the door as I rush out of the room.

"Are you okay?" Barrett asks as he enters the house.

I go hot all over.

"What are we having for dinner?" I ask and head to the kitchen, keeping myself as far apart from him as the house will allow.

I open the fridge, and for the first few seconds take in cold air, while pretending to scope it out.

I feel Barret come up behind me. His hands touch the sides of my shoulders.

I want to lean back and have his arms wrap around me. We're married after all. That would be perfectly normal.

"I'll cook today. Sit and rest."

I blink. Barret steers me toward the kitchen table.

I sink into a chair and pretend to watch the orange and pink glow of the setting sun through the kitchen window.

Barret gets ingredients, chops them, and starts cooking something. Once I feel safe he's concentrating on his task, my eyes wander back to him, tracking his every movement.

For such a big man, he's agile and graceful when he moves, which is so unlike clumsy me. He cooks like someone who's been doing something for a long time and can do it with their eyes closed. His butt looks good in the jeans he changed into and his back and arm muscles ripple as he reaches for utensils.

"Like what you see?"

"What do you mean?" I play with the crochet patterns on the tablecloth. "This is pretty. Who made it?"

"My granny. She used patterns from tablecloths my great grannies used but were too old to carry on using." He places a salad on the table.

"Really? It must bring you such a sense of belonging. I love that."

"Change whatever you want, to make the place into something you like."

If he keeps being this generous, it won't be long before I'm completely in love with him. "The dress I wore today was my mom's wedding dress. She's much slimmer than me, so the seamstress used the cloth below the knees to enlarge the sides to fit me. I love knowing others, especially people I love have used whatever I'm wearing."

"You were sexy in it. I bet the thoughts going through your mind when you were eying me a little while ago don't come close to the ones I had when I saw you in that gorgeous dress." Barret says. Then he turns and heads for the cooker.

I'm so glad he's not looking at me right now. I'm as pleased as a schoolgirl being told by her prom date that she's stunning.

He finds me attractive. At the very least, he thinks I was attractive in my wedding dress.

That makes me bold. I watch him until he brings

two steaming plates of stew to the table. We eat mostly in silence. At first, I'm a little worried Barrett is bored and am tempted to make casual conversation, but I decide to behave the way I usually do. That's what we agreed on. To be ourselves, to not try to be something other than what we are.

Then, I realize the silence is comfortable. We both have another more stew. When I finish that, I sip wine as he polishes off another plate.

I insist on washing up, still, Barrett decides to help by rinsing.

"They'll air dry," he says as I grab a dishcloth.

"Can we sit outside for a bit?"

Barrett grabs the bottle of wine, a beer, and a blanket. I take my wine glass and follow him out and around the porch to the back of the cabin until we reach a porch seat.

My mouth opens as I spy the view ahead. A mountain slope and trees rise toward the dark sky. The soft noise of babbling reaches my ears, but I can't see any water.

"Is there a stream nearby?"

He points to his left. I don't see it at first. When I do, I'm awed again. I've seen nothing more picturesque.

"You must sit here every day. I've been staring for only what must be a few minutes and I feel the tranquility of the mountain."

"Most days. It's not always tranquil though."

We sit and appreciate the view.

"Some visitors to the lodge further up the mountain can be loud."

"Is that the generator? I know you explained about electricity and internet out here but I'm still surprised you have decent Wi-Fi." I point to a large device.

Barrett made sure I knew about the difficulties I might face living out here.

"We use it if there's a power cut. With an external antenna installed, Wi-Fi is not too bad."

Barrett spreads the blanket over my knees. "Even though it's summer, up here, it gets a little chilly at night."

We sit down and peer at the mountain. I can feel Barrett sitting close to me and hear the lulling sound of the stream. I'm both comforted and on edge, my body alive and full of anticipation.

CHAPTER FOUR

Barrett

I REMOVE THE wineglass from Keisha's limp hand and place it on the floor. She's just as striking with her eyes closed as she's awake.

She's leaning back against the bench and snoring lightly. Unbidden, my hand reaches toward her face. I stop it before it can trace her lips and touch her face.

I shake my head. It's been too long since I got laid. I must be needing the warmth the body of a woman can provide. And Keisha is my type of woman.

Carefully, I lift her. This close, it's not just her mint scent I can smell. Something else stirs my nose. A fragrance that must be all Keisha–feminine and earthy.

Carrying a woman shouldn't be this good. Keisha feels right in my arms, as if she's meant to be held by me alone. She doesn't wake as I enter the house, the bedroom, and sit down so I can pull back the sheets on her side of the bed.

Even when I stand up and walk round to place her on the bed, she sleeps like a baby. I lay her down and cover her before I head out of the room, collect the glasses from the porch and shut the cabin down for the night.

In the bedroom, I strip off my shirt in the soft light of the moon, but at the moment my hands reach for the zipper on my jeans, I pause. I don't want Keisha to be startled if she wakes and finds herself sleeping with a naked man. Even if that man is her husband. I can sleep in my jeans for one night.

I slip into bed, fold my hands and tuck them under my head. So much for my well-laid plan. I look at Keisha again, but she's still sleeping soundly. I'll just have to start it tomorrow.

She's lying so close to me it's fucking hard not to reach out and touch her. I really don't know how I'll cope tomorrow night when I execute my plan for day one and hold her in my arms.

***

THE SUN IS shining brightly and soaking the cabin and farm in its hot rays. Keisha comes out of the house and stands on the porch, her face turned upward. I stop throwing chicken feed and watch as she stretches, tits straining against her blouse.

She spots me and drops her arms. She's a little shy and I'm perverted enough to like it. I watch her walk toward me, hips swaying tantalizingly.

"I'm sorry I fell asleep on our wedding night."

She's worrying that gorgeous bottom lip again. I feast my eyes for another beat.

"We have today."

"Right." She looks at the chickens as if she's never seen hens before. "What can I do? I saw the note you left about starting the chores and made breakfast."

"Let's eat."

Inside the house, I wash up while Keisha dishes bacon, eggs and sausages.

"I'll go out with you and learn the chores." Keisha says once I'm back in the kitchen.

I nod and tuck into the food she made. "How do you feel? Did you sleep well?"

She gives me a sideways glance, then focuses on her food. "I've already apologized for falling asleep."

A chuckle erupts out of me. She's so easy to tease. "Keisha, you had a hard, long day. It isn't every day a woman gets married, especially a marriage like ours. Even if it's something you wanted to do, I'm sure you had a few worries. It couldn't have been easy trusting a man you've never met. I really want to know if you were okay sleeping in a strange bed."

"I guess I'm a little embarrassed." She tucks hairs that escaped her ponytail behind her ears. "Usually, I have a hard time falling asleep in unknown places. I must have been more exhausted than I thought I was because the last thing I remembered when I got up was taking in that scenic view last night."

We finish our meal and while she's doing dishes; I get a gift-wrapped box from the bedroom.

"What is it?" She asks as I hand it to her.

"Put them on. They aren't pretty, but will keep your feet safer than your sneakers."

As she opens the box and puts on the boots I gifted her, I grab jugs and a pair of gloves.

"Thank you! They feel comfortable."

Warmth spreads all over me.

"I got your shoe size from the information the matchmaking agency sent."

Needing cool air, I head outside. When Keisha joins me, I give her a tour of the farm and explain the different chores that need doing. Her dark brown eyes are enormous and she stops me to ask questions.

I collected eggs earlier, but there are a few more in the nesting boxes, so I take those out.

"I didn't realize how big the farm is. There are so many chickens. What do you do with the eggs?"

"The bakery in town takes half of them, and the rest go to the restaurants and local shops."

Her eyes widen even more when we reach the vegetable garden and I remember she mentioned a love of gardening.

"Can we harvest some vegetables?"

She's so excited, I can't help laughing. "This

afternoon. I guess this can be one of your chores."

I shepherd her toward the goats. "These beauties are going to be cranky if I don't milk them now."

"This is Angelina." I march the goat toward the stand and milk her.

"How do you know?" Keisha peers at the goat.

"See this black dot on her nose?"

Keisha nods.

"Seraphina and Isabella don't have it."

"Let me try," Keisha says after she's watched me milk Seraphina.

She grabs Isabella, the youngest goat, and shepherds her out of the goat pen like I did.

"She's following me!"

I help her put the goat in the stand when the latch doesn't close properly.

"It isn't coming out," she says after a few pulls on Isabella's udder.

I place my hands on hers and guide the movement of her fingers.

"It's working!"

There are small flecks of gold in Keisha's eyes.

That unfamiliar feeling is back. Whatever the hell it is, has my heart pounding. I can't tear my eyes away from Keisha's innocent, delighted face.

"Let me try by myself," she says, and the spell is broken.

I blink and slip my fingers away.

She's focused on what she's doing and looks as

excited as a kid who's learned to ride a bike for the first time. The milk is coming in spurts, but I can tell that with a little more practice, she'll do a great job.

We have lunch and spend the afternoon doing more chores. She's eager to help but, by the time we seat to eat the stew I warmed up for us, I can tell she's going to be sore tomorrow.

"When did you make all this delicious food?" She fails to hide a yawn.

"My cooking is not nearly as delicious as this. Mr. Jackson, a friend of Dad's, gave it to me a couple of days ago. I'll introduce you when we go into town."

"From Jackson's Diner?"

How did she know?

Keisha laughs. "Did you know you raise your left eyebrow if something surprises you?"

"It's a habit I can't seem to shake."

"Jackson's Diner is one of the most visited places in Blossom Ford, Arizona," she announces. "I wanted to find out a bit more about the place I'd be living in and did some research."

"You worked hard today!"

"Do I get a reward?"

Hot damn! She may be thinking of an innocent reward, yet my mind conjures a different picture.

I must have given something away because the amusement in her eyes is replaced by awareness.

"Later. In a few days." I meant to whisper it, but a growl emerges instead.

Keisha bites her bottom lip, then tucks into her food.

She lasts an hour outside before she admits she has to turn in. I do a round of the farm while she readies for bed. By the time I enter the bedroom, she's lying down.

I smile when she blinks up at the ceiling. She's trying so hard to stay awake. I strip, place my clothes on the rocking chair in the room's corner and pad to the bed. Keisha is staring at my cock. It stirs, as if inviting her gaze, and I realize how much I enjoy her watching me. I get into bed and look at her.

"Come here. Let me hug you."

She slides closer and lays her head on my chest. I wrap my arms around her and pull her slightly up my body.

"Comfortable?"

"Yes."

I frown at how low her voice is. She wrote no to the virgin question on the agency's questionnaire.

"I sleep with my birthday costume on. Does it make you uncomfortable?"

A head shake.

I rub one hand up and down the silky material covering her back. It's so good to have her pressed against the side of my body.

"For the next few days, I'm just going to hug you like this. It'll give us some time to get to know each other. Tell me if you feel uncomfortable."

"I like this," Keisha's voice is stronger this time.

"So do I."

It's the sweetest torture I've ever felt. She must be wearing shorts because I can feel the soft skin of her legs as they lay beside mine. I breathe in and out steadily and try not to think about the softness of her tits, squashed against my side.

"Goodnight sweetheart." I kiss her forehead.

She's tense for a moment, then relaxes.

"Goodnight Barrett!

Three days. My plan is to give her three days to settle down on the farm and get used to being together before we have sex. This is only the first night and I'm already fucked. I want to rip her clothes and eat her up until she's screaming with pleasure.

CHAPTER FIVE

Keisha

I'VE BEEN AT the farm for four days and have already fallen in love with the vegetable garden, the animals and the mountain. This morning I only felt a few twinges in my body, so even the pain I had after helping with the chores the first couple of days has subsided. The only problem? I'm falling in love with the farm owner.

We've settled into a nice routine. Barrett wakes up at the crack of dawn and starts working. I make breakfast about an hour later and we eat together before I help on the farm. I return to the cabin to make lunch and sometimes we have that outside.

I help a little more in the afternoons before showering and cooking dinner.

It's late afternoon now. My hair is tied up in a towel

and I'm finishing dinner when Barrett walks in the door. He glances at my bare legs. I swear I can see heat in his eyes before he turns and heads to the bathroom.

I don't know what's going through his mind. He looks at me like a man starved of sex one minute, the next he's like the Santas Mom and Dad used to take me to when I was little; all sweet, kind, and cuddly.

I lay the table and dish up. By the time I'm finished, Barrett is in the kitchen, the combination of his wet hair and beard, citrus shower gel scent and low-slung pants making my mouth water.

After dinner, Barrett grabs my glass of wine and a beer for him.

"I have to do my hair. I'll stay here."

Barrett freezes. "Why?"

"It goes everywhere. And I have to moisturize it. You might not like that."

"I won't know until I see it," he says after studying me for what feels like ages.

I shrug, grab my comb, moisturizer, and a couple of scrunchies and head outside. His beer and my glass of wine are on the floor beside the seat. He has a can of beer every night. I guess the hard work of the farm takes care of the calories he ingests.

I can only hope that the physical labor I'm doing will offset the daily glass of wine I've been drinking.

I unwrap the towel and rub it around my head. My hair takes forever to dry. Barrett is staring at it. I can't tell if he's shocked. My long, silky, pressed hair is gone.

In its place is a mass of tight curls.

I warned him.

I part a small section of it and pat dry the ends.

"Can I do that?"

I gawk at him.

"It's got to be easier if I do it, right?"

I hold out the towel.

When he takes it, I sit cross-legged on the floor.

"Where do you want to sit?" I ask when Barrett stands beside me.

He takes my spot on the bench. I feel his hands on my head and ready myself for the sting of pulled hair.

"You're gentler than my mom," I say after he's done nearly half of my head. His hands are massive, I didn't expect him to be so gentle.

"Did she do your hair like this?"

"When I was very little. One day she wasn't well. Dad had to do it. His braids weren't as pretty as Mom's, but his hands were gentler. From then on, I threw a tantrum if Mom tried to do it."

"I can't imagine that."

Now I know his voice well enough, to make out he's amused.

"I was very bratty before Mom and Dad divorced."

Barrett is quiet for a moment. "I'm guessing it wasn't amicable."

Now it's my turn to be amused by the caution in his voice. This is why I'm falling for him. There's a gentleness in him I didn't really expect. He's perceptive, too.

"It was hell. I was twelve and couldn't understand why our happy world was collapsing." I hug my knees and stare at the wilderness of the mountain. "But now they are the best of friends. Mom met and married a Spanish man shortly after. It took Dad a couple of years to date again. He's married and has two kids. It wasn't until they were both happy that I realized their new partners suit them better."

"Who did you live with?"

"Dad. Until I finished high school and started working. Then he and my stepmom moved up North to be closer to her family."

"It's done," Barrett says.

He hands me the comb and shifts back to his place.

I moisturize and quickly make two French braids, conscious of Barrett watching my hands as he drinks chilled beer.

"Are you trying to learn to braid?"

"Yes. We may have a girl. She might prefer my hands."

I'm in love with this man.

There's no more avoiding it. I've fallen for the way he holds me and makes me feel safe. The way he looks out and cares for me. At that moment, I'm sure if we have children, he'll do everything to protect and keep them safe.

If only he's as eager as me to start on childbearing, everything would be perfect.

"What was that?"

Heat races all over my body. Did I say that aloud?

"Nothing." I stand. "I'm going to turn in."

I can't make out the expression in Barrett's eyes.

I gather my things and go into the house. I wear a camisole and short set I got especially for after the wedding and get into bed, thinking about when Barrett is planning on having a child. Perhaps I need to be more proactive and start things?

The door swings open. I watch Barrett as he strips and pads toward me. My womb clenches, my nipples harden. His size doesn't surprise me anymore, but I can't help wondering again if he'll fit inside me. The fact that he's aware of my scrutiny turns me on even more. I love cuddling up to his hard, hot body, but it's no longer enough.

How does a wife ask her husband for sex?

"Do you want to sleep?" Barrett says as he gets into bed.

"No!"

He leans over me and caresses my bottom lip with the tip of one finger.

I suck my breath.

His finger presses along the seam of my lips. When I open my mouth a little, he slides his finger in. I pull on it. Darts of pleasure shoot to my core.

"Keisha, I want to fuck the hell out of you!"

Barrett's growl makes me wet. I have no problem making out the expression in his eyes now. I wrap my arms around his neck and pull him down.

He kisses me hard, his tongue dueling against mine. It's just what I'm craving.

His enormous hands tug at the bottom of my top and slide it up my chest. I lift and let him take it off me.

"Ah sweetheart." He stares at my breasts then palms them.

"These fit in my hands." He squeezes them so they push together, his big thumbs caressing my pebbled nipples.

I moan.

He plays with my nipples, first licking, then suckling them until I think I'm going to orgasm.

"Barrett." It's a hoarse whisper.

"What?"

He blows on my breasts, the cool air making my puckered nipples harder. My hips lift of their own accord.

"Barrett?"

"Tell me."

He slides down my body, grabs my shorts and panties, and rips them.

"You're so pretty, Keisha. I'm going to love eating this pussy."

My hips lift again. My tongue moistens my dry lips.

"Say it Sweetheart. What do you want?"

"Touch me there."

I don't care anymore how embarrassing asking him to touch and kiss my private parts is. I need relief now.

"That's it, Sweetheart."

Barrett's hand snakes past my bare mound and flicks the top of my clit. He strokes the opening of my pussy.

"I love how wet you are."

With his slippery fingers, he rubs my clit, their roughness and his speed providing the right pressure. I grip the sheets as tension mounts in my core and reaches an unbearable point. My pussy contracts and explodes, tipping me over the edge, and I explode.

Barrett tongues my juices and aftershocks quake through me.

He slides up my body, kisses my breasts, then the side of my neck.

"That was part of your reward," his whisper is rough against my ear.

I barely have time to work out what he means before I feel his cock pushing against my slippery entrance.

I slip my hand between our bodies and stroke up and down his thick cock before guiding him into me.

He hisses and bites my neck.

Moisture seeps out of me.

Then he's stretching me. I inhale and he pauses, breathing hard. He growls words that flush my entire body and turn me on.

Soon, I'm ready for more of him and lift my hips. His big cock surges a little further into me again and again until it's buried to the hilt.

Initially, Barrett sets a languid pace. His hands rove over my body and he bites my earlobes till I'm undulating against him. Then he grabs my butt and fucks me hard, his hard, long pennis driving in and out of me until I'm keening his name.

He rubs my clit, and I contract around him, screaming in pleasure.

Barrett growls and spills hot seed into me. When he's still, he flips us so I'm lying on top of him, in the position we slept in since our wedding day.

As pleasure aftershocks ripple through my body and Barrett's big hand slides up and down my back, a question rises in my mind, even as my eyes flutter close.

Will I be able to keep my feelings hidden from my husband?

CHAPTER SIX

Barrett

IT'S A WEEK since Keisha and I slept together, and I can't remember a time I was happier. We work hard during the day, then fuck harder at night. She may not have had a lot of experience in the bedroom, but she meets every rough demand I make.

I pop my head out of a chicken coop and peer at the thick drops of rain pounding the yard. Even though I'm wearing a sturdy anorak and knee-high waterproof boots, the heavy rain found a way into my clothes.

The cabin door crashes open. Keisha stares out, then screams and dashes into the rain before I can holler at her to head back inside. I search for whatever alarmed her, my body coiled to spring into action.

Then I see the fox. I barrel down the yard toward Keisha, but it's too late.

She swings a broom toward the animal, yelling. It yelps and turns, then shrieks at Keisha, who swings the broom again.

My heart drops as Keisha loses her footing and falls. I miss her by a second.

"Are you okay?"

My heart is in my mouth as I look her over, checking she has hurt nothing.

"There's a fox." She tries to sit, but I stop her.

"It's gone."

"What about the chicken? Is it okay? The fox almost got it."

"For fuck's sake, Keisha! Will you lie still?"

She blinks up at me.

"Can you move your toes? And fingers?"

"Yes."

I carry her into the cabin and sit her down.

"I'm dropping mud on the chair. Let me clean up."

I stop her and crouch in front of her.

"Don't you ever do that again? Do you hear me?"

Keisha stares at me.

"Tell me you'll never put yourself in danger like that again. Not for anyone or anything?"

She nods.

I pull her down onto my lap and wrap my arms around her. Only when I feel the warmth of her soft body, does my heart slow down and I realize Keisha's patting my back.

"Barrett, we have to wash the mud off."

I take her into the shower, strip us down, and rinse the mud off. When we're both dry and dressed, I make her a hot chocolate.

"I'm going out for a bit," I say once she sips the sweet, dark brown liquid.

"In this rain?"

"I know these roads like the back of my hand. I'm used to driving in this weather, too."

"Let me get my anorak. I'll come with you."

I wrap a blanket around her.

"Stay warm."

Then I grab the truck key and flee the cabin. I drive down the mountain, slower than usual, because no matter what I told Keisha, it's dangerous to drive on the mountain roads while it's raining this hard.

Halfway down the mountain, I stop, slam out of the truck, and scream. I can't believe I've gone and fallen in love. I've done the very thing that made Dad's life a misery.

The worst thing is I've been lying to myself. I've been falling for her ever since I saw her through the window, when the train stopped outside Blossom Ford Station. I'm fascinated by her determination and courage, the way she works so damn hard even though she doesn't have to, and how she gives herself wholeheartedly to me.

Seeing her in danger only made me admit the truth.

I'm hopelessly in love with my wife.

I get back in the truck. Having to use all of my senses

to prevent an accident stops me from thinking about Keisha, so I drive down the rest of the mountain.

Outside O'Connors, I pull up. I desperately want the alcohol induced oblivion that I can find inside the bar, but I have to drive up the mountain. It's only four in the afternoon but no taxi will take me up there and I don't want to leave Keisha alone tonight. My friend Verlin is the only person who'd drive me up without a single question. It's a shame he's out of town.

A horn beeps behind me. It's old Jackson. He drives off and I follow him.

"What are you doing outside in this rain?" He asks when we are sitting in a booth in the diner after he's sent the waitress home.

The place is dead. It's no surprise, the way it's raining.

"Married life mistreating you already?"

Most people saw the grumpy and rough exterior of old man Jackson and mistakenly judged him mean. But he's the kindest man I know. And he's sort of a second dad. Now and then, someone would say they saw Mom in some town and Dad would go searching for her. Until the age of eleven, I stayed with old man Jackson. After that, I took care of myself at home.

"Did Dad ever regret loving Mom?"

He narrows his eyes on me, bushy gray brows almost joining. "No."

My lip curls up.

"Some men will love two or three times, others love

once. No matter how painful it is, it's a miracle to care for someone more than you do for yourself."

Is he talking about himself? As far as I know, only Dad, Verlin, and I know he's been in love with Mrs. Gallagher ever since she came to town as a young bride. Verlin and I overheard him talking with Dad.

Even though Mrs. Gallagher has been a widow for over thirty years, they are just friends. He won't say anything because he believes she's still in love with her dead husband.

"Some women are meant for the mountain, others are not, no matter how much they love their husbands. Have you talked to Keisha? I may be wrong, but I think she's the type that'll stay."

He's an excellent judge of character; I desperately want to believe him. I introduced Keisha to him a couple of days ago when we came down the mountain to deliver eggs.

I want to tell him to confess to Mrs. Gallagher, but I know better. He'll be mortified if I bring it up. It's better if he isn't aware Verlin and I know his secret.

"You better get back, it's getting dark. It'll be even harder to drive in this weather. Unless you want to kip down here tonight."

"Keisha's too new to the mountain. She'll be worried if I don't get back."

old man Jackson cracks up. The sound is gravelly. Whilst I was younger, I used to wonder if that was because he rarely laughed and so his laughing muscles were rusty.

"What's so funny?"

"You remind me of the old times with your dad. When we were younger."

"I'm leaving."

More laughter.

"Tell that O'Connor boy to stop sending me those bloody supplements. I'm not that old yet."

"Which one?"

"How the fuck should I know? There are so many of them."

Out of the nine O'Connors in Blossom Ford, Verlin is the only one who'd dare send supplements to old man Jackson. The old man knew that too.

I wave goodbye and sprint to the truck. It's a long drive back to the cabin. By the time I arrive, it's past dinnertime.

Keisha stands at the door, wrapped up in the blanket I gave her earlier.

God, I love her.

I don't know about tomorrow, but right now, I feel blessed I've had the chance to love her. Even as the realization crashes through me, a horrifying thought shoots its insidious claws into me.

What will I do if she ever wants to leave?

CHAPTER SEVEN

Keisha

BARRETT HAS NOT been the same since the day that damn fox snuck in our yard. That was four days ago. He's brooding over something, but won't tell me what it is.

He's silent. Not Barrett silent, this is uncomfortable. I miss making love with him and his arms around me as we go to sleep. I can see he still cares for me in the way he'll pick up a heavy load from me and carry it or when he slips a blanket over my shoulders while we sit outside.

However, he's staying outside longer. Yesterday, he went to the yard after dinner and didn't come in until I was in bed.

I bite my lip as he comes in. He takes me silently, then heads for the bathroom. I tell myself he's checking

I'm okay, nevertheless the tension is getting to me.

Dinner is uncomfortable again.

"What's wrong? I've already said I'll be more careful, so what happened that day doesn't happen again. I don't know what to do to make things right."

I can't stand how awkward we've become around each other.

"You've done nothing wrong. Give me a few days."

Cold fills the pit of my stomach. I've had the "it's me, not you" talk before. I thought Barrett was better, that he'd at least be honest with me, but I've been wrong before.

"If you found someone else, just tell me."

I hate the whine I hear in my voice. Hate the pain that's already ripping through me because no matter how much it tears me apart, I won't stay with a cheating man.

"Christ, Keisha! What the hell are you talking about?"

I swallow.

"Maybe you tired of my body. I know some men find it a novelty to be with plus sized women, but they go back to being with slender women when the novelty wears off."

"What prick spouted that nonsense at you?"

He shoves his chair back, comes round, and grabs my hand.

"What are you going to do? Let me go."

He marches us into the bedroom, shoves everything

away from the center of the dresser and stands in front of the mirror there.

"Strip!"

"Barrett, what are you doing?"

"Do it now Keisha, or I'm ripping those clothes off you."

His shirt is on the floor. He removes his pants and underpants as I hesitate over my bra.

Quickly, I pull my shorts down.

"Come here."

Just like that, I'm ready for him. My core clenches and moisture seeps into my panties.

I close the space between us.

"What do you see?"

I clear my throat twice before I can speak. "You're hard."

"I'm so fucking hard, I'm worried I'm going to cream myself before I pleasure you. Who made my cock that way?"

I glance at him. Fire glazes his eyes, the way it does when he's making love to me.

"Keisha?" He growls.

"Me?"

I'm getting wetter.

"DAMN RIGHT! KEISHA MADE MY COCK AS HARD AS A STEEL ROD."

He grips my shoulders and forces me to turn around, so I'm facing the mirror.

"Wrap your arms around my neck."

"Let's get into bed."

It's one thing for him to see me, but it's another for me to see myself like this.

"No."

I hesitate.

Barrett waits, fiery eyes watching me through the mirror.

I'm too turned on to stop. I wrap my arms around his neck, my fingers brushing against the hair at his nape.

He rips my bra. Then my panties. His eyes don't leave me the whole time. Mine widen as I realize my heart is racing. I can hardly catch my breath.

"See how beautiful your tits are?" He pushes them together, kneading them. "I'll never tire of petting them. Look, Keisha."

I let my gaze wander from the hard planes of his face and the heat in his eyes to my body.

"This is one of my favorite colors." He touches my dark aureoles with his thumbs, still massaging my breasts.

I gasp. They are my breasts, but I don't recognize how arousing they look, thrusting forward against his palms, my nipples as hard as pebbles.

He splays his hand on the swell of my tummy. "I love how soft you are here."

His cock pushes against my back. It's slippery, as if pre-cum is leaking out of it.

"Tilt your hips forward."

I want his fingers down there. But when I obey him, he leans over me and slides his palms up my thighs.

"Your curvy legs are another favorite of mine."

My eyes follow his every movement. The contrast of my darker body against his lighter one fascinates me.

Finally, his hand touches my clit.

"Tilt a little more."

With two fingers, he spreads my nether lips so the dark little mass that is my engorged clit is clearly visible.

"See? You have the prettiest pussy I've ever seen. You're so wet and pink. Oh, God Keisha, I want to take you now."

He pushes against me. Simultaneously, his fingers stroke me.

I pant and move against him, throwing my head back. I feel so good, I can't keep my eyes open anymore.

Barrett licks my neck, and I convulse. My legs give way, but he holds me. He lays me over the dresser, anchoring my arms there.

In one smooth movement, he enters me.

"Sweet Keisha," he growls.

"I wish you could see how gorgeous your curvy ass is, with me working it as I slide in and out of you."

"I feel it. Barrett, it's so good."

He freezes.

"Don't stop."

"Who's the most beautiful girl in my world?"

"Keisha." I push my butt against him. "Don't stop."

"Say it like you mean it. Who's my girl?" He roars.

"Keisha!"

"I love every part of you, Keisha." He punctuates each word with a thrust so hard my body slides forward on the dresser.

I'm crying now.

"I love you Keisha."

I turn my head so I can see him. "I love you too, Barrett."

He bucks into me, shooting semen up my pussy, and I come again in the most powerful orgasm of my life.

I don't know how long we stay here, panting. After a little while, Barrett lifts me to the bed, holding me in our familiar position.

"I'm destroying our contract. If you try to leave me, I'm going to lock you up and find ways to change your mind," Barrett says.

I lift my head, pet his face and beard.

He tells me about his mom leaving.

My heart breaks for the little boy he was. I rub my face on his chest.

"I no longer want or need that contract. I love my life here with you, Barrett. I love you. I even love Angelina, Seraphina and Isabella. And to me, marriage means forever."

"Good. Because you were made for my hands, my mouth and my cock, Keisha. And I was made for every sexy part of you."

EPILOGUE

Barrett

Eight Years Later

I'M AT THE stream we can see from our house, trying to stay upright as my three kids use all their combined forces to topple me. I roar as I pretend to be a human-stealing beast.

"Give back our sister, you mean troll," Blake shouts. He's only seven, but his body is strong like mine was when I was his age. He yanks my right leg.

His brother, four-year-old Malik, tries to pull my other leg but keeps on falling.

I lift each leg in turns, making it look as if they are gaining ground. It's hard not to laugh because Little Destiny, who's sitting on my shoulders, is giggling when she should be terrified.

"Malik, pull harder, he's nearly down," Blake

shouts.

I bend my knees and drop to the soft grass, careful not to let Destiny fall.

"Daddy, higher," she says.

"I have a cookie in my pocket, Destiny." Tony reaches for his sister, who's now desperate to fall into his arms.

I struggle a little more, then put my baby girl on my chest, fall back and allow her brothers to steal her from me.

"I'll live happily with you, Mr. Monster," Keisha drops beside me.

I put my arm around her, and we watch the kids play.

"Let's have more picnic days like this. We can afford to hire help."

"They are growing too fast. I can't believe Destiny is two. It seems like only yesterday; you were giving birth to her."

"Don't remind me."

"I've been keeping my eye out for someone I can trust and will do a good job, and I believe I found someone. I can't wait to take you on our honeymoon."

"Without the kids?"

"You don't think they'll be okay with Ella, your mom or dad?"

Keisha and Ella have become such good friends. We babysit for her and her husband August and reciprocate sleep overs.

"It's not that. I just think it might be weird to be apart from them for more than a day."

"I know what you mean," I say.

I love my life with Keisha and my boys and girl so much. I feel like the luckiest man on earth. It's a miracle that Keisha, who loves this mountain like I do, came into my life.

"I still want to go," Keisha says.

"Any particular place?"

We've talked about going on our honeymoon before, but never really nailed down a place.

"Let's talk about it on the porch tonight, when the kids are sleeping. I think they're getting puckish now."

I sit up. Sure enough, they are heading for the picnic Keisha laid out.

"Let's feed our family," I say.

I pull her up and hold her hand as we walk toward our babies.

The End

MATCHED TO PATRICK

THE O'CONNORS OF BLOSSOM FORD #1

Patrick

MINGLED LAUGHTER DRIFTS from the sitting room, bringing mixed feelings of joy and sadness. We decorated the entire house in green–it's St Patrick's Day. As usual, we've been to church and are now having beef pot roast, which Mom and Aunt Shauna insist on making every year on the feast day of St. Patrick. Dad would have been so happy to hear that laughter. Even though we gathered like today at Christmas, St Patrick's Day was his favorite holiday.

I remove more salad from the refrigerator.

"Ready for the parade of women our moms no doubt have lined up for you this year?" My cousin Lorcan asks. I know his lilting voice like I know my own.

I snap the refrigerator closed. "Will I be the only one

on display?"

He winces. "You're the eldest. And you're Aunt Caitlin's only son, so you'll definitely be in the firing line. Mom will surely want to marry Riordan off first. I'll be an afterthought."

The lump in my throat prevents me from chuckling. I can't really blame Lorcan. I used to be like him. The thought of marriage drove me barmy. Not anymore.

At first I couldn't imagine myself being happy with a family, not with the crushing guilt I felt over what happened to Little Fiona. Before Dad passed, he made me promise to let go of that guilt and cherish the time I've been blessed with. Although I believed it'd never happen, little by little, I'm appreciating life.

I want what Mom and Dad had, though. They were meant for each other. Someone out there is my soulmate and the moment I find her, I'm not letting go. For the last couple of years, Mom and Aunt Shauna's matchmaking efforts haven't bothered me in the least.

I glance outside to where Riordan, my cousin and Lorcan's eldest brother, sits in the spring sun. "Riordan is not ready to get married. I doubt he'll hang around for the picnic and anyone our moms might want to set him up with."

That giant of a man is still blaming himself for what happened to his little sister Fiona, even though it's been twenty-six years since she was taken from us. Our dads were first cousins -both O'Connors. The two of us are forty-four, but I'm older than Riordan by one week. As the oldest children in the O'Connor family, it was our responsibility to make sure Fiona was safe.

Lorcan opens the back door.

"Mom is calling," he says to Rio.

It's the only thing that'll move my eldest cousin. Aunt Shauna may not be calling him now, but Riordan knows she'll soon be, wanting to make sure he spends as much time with us as possible before he scoots up the mountain.

Riordan and Lorcan's six brothers and Dad are watching TV while Mom and Aunt Shauna are chat.

"Don't forget to take good care of my friend Nara when she gets here. She was very kind to me the other day in town when I forgot my wallet," Mom reminds me.

We spend another couple of hours leisurely drinking and chatting, then get up to prepare for the outdoor picnic, which starts at four. The whole town is invited to our farm. Our parents started the tradition a few years after settling in Blossom Ford and starting a lettuce farm together, because they missed spending St Patrick's Day with their large family back in Ireland.

We put up tents on the large grass area between my house and Riordan's. Mom and Aunt Shauna used to do all the food when they were younger, but now, Lorcan gets caterers in to bring sandwiches and other finger food. By the time the townsfolk arrive, Cormac and Emmet, my youngest cousins, have set up a DJ stand which is playing upbeat music and the entire field is filled with green bunting and balloons.

I'm taking a breather from greeting people when I see a woman strolling towards Mom. Something about the way she walks catches my attention. She's wearing black skinny jeans that mold her curvy ass to perfection and a light green top that covers a pair of generous breasts and complements the sun-kissed tone of her skin. Wavy jet-black hair falls below her shoulders and shimmers in the sun.

I'm too far away to see the color of her eyes. Before I know it, I'm marching towards Mom, curiosity and something I can't name, compelling me forward.

"I'm so glad you came, Nara," Mom is saying when I reach her side on a strategic part of the field where she, Aunt Shauna, and their friend Ms. Penny can see everyone.

Tawny, that's the color of her eyes.

I answer myself as Nara greets everyone with an amiable smile that reaches her almond-shaped, yellow-brown eyes and warms the inside of my chest. She's comfortable around Mom, Aunt Shauna and their friends, even though she must be in her mid-twenties. The silver hoops on the tops of her ears glint in the sunshine.

"This is my son, Patrick." Mom points to me.

I stretch out my hand in greeting and when she holds mine; hers is small and smooth against my large and calloused one. I don't let go and she glances up at me.

That's when I know. That I've found the woman I've spent the last few years searching for.

The friendly warmth on her face is replaced by something else: interest. A tinge of pink fills her cheeks before she pulls her hand away.

Her voice cracks a little when she says hello leaving me to wonder where the confidence she exhibited a few moments ago went.

"I'll show you where the food is," I say.

"I don't want to trouble you." She looks about her. "I'll find it, thank you."

"It's no trouble at all," Mom beams at Nara. "Patrick will walk you over to the food area. Just ask him if there's anything you need to know."

A frown forms on my face as I lead the way. At my age, I'm old enough to know when a woman has the hots for me. I know Nara fancies me, but she's decided not to pursue it.

If there's one thing I'm good at, is getting to the root of a problem. Now I've found Nara, I'll have to convince her I'm the only man for her.

OTHER BOOKS BY THE AUTHOR

CURVY BRIDES OF BLOSSOM FORD SERIES

MARRYING THE PROTECTIVE PROFESSOR

MARRYING THE GRUMPY DIRECTOR

MARRYING THE POSSESSIVE NEIGHBOR

MARRYING THE WIDOWED DOCTOR

MARRYING THE SCARRED SOLDIER

MARRYING THE OBSESSIVE CEO

MARRYING THE BIG MOUNTAIN MAN

THE O'CONNORS OF BLOSSOM FORD SERIES

MATCHED TO PATRICK

REDEEMING THE MOUNTAIN MAN

ABOUT THE AUTHOR

Iris West writes short and spicy romance about alpha heroes and the women they can't help falling in love with. She loves reading all types of romance books that have a happy ending and is an avid Kdrama fan.

Follow or like her on Facebook and Goodreads.

FREE BOOK

Would you like a free book? Sign up to my mailing list at https://dl.bookfunnel.com/t191w45ryj to receive a copy of Loving My Fake Husband, a free to subscribers only, Curvy Brides of Blossom Ford Series short story.

HELP OTHERS FIND THIS BOOK

Thank you for reading Marrying The Big Mountain Man. If you enjoyed this book, please help others discover it by leaving a review at your favorite online book store.

Many thanks,

Iris xx